Adding It Up

WILLITS BRANCH LIBRARY

BASED ON **TIMOTHY GOES TO SCHOOL** AND OTHER STORIES BY

ROSEMARY WELLS

ILLUSTRATED BY MICHAEL KOELSCH

VIKING

Cover and interior illustrations copyright © Rosemary Wells, 2001 • Interior illustrations by Michael Koelsch • Text copyright © Penguin Putnam Inc., 2001
Educational consultant: John F. Savage, Ed.D. • All rights reserved • Library of Congress Catalog Card Number: 2001002316 • ISBN: 0-670-03519-X

Mrs. Jenkins's Class,

Mrs. JENKINS

TIMOTHY

FRITZ

YOKO

CHARLES

Hilltop School

1 2 3 4 5 6 7 8 9 10

"Good morning, class," says Mrs. Jenkins. "Today we are going to practice counting. I know you can all count to 10. Who can count to 20?"

"I can," says Timothy. "1, 2, 3, 4, 5, 6, 7, 8, 9, 10, 11, 12, 13, 14, 15, 16, 17, 18, 19, 20."

"Very good," says Mrs. Jenkins. "Does anyone know what number comes next?"

"I do," says Yoko. "21."

"You're right," says Mrs. Jenkins. "Let's keep going. How high can you count?"

Can you count to 20? Can you count higher than 20? Count as high as you can. Now look at the number line below. Can you say which numbers are missing?

11 _ 13 _ _ 16 _ 18 _ 20

The Next Step

Once you know how to count 20, it's not too hard to learn to count all the way to 100! How high can you count?

11 12 13 14 15 16 17 18 19 **20**

"Numbers are all around us," says Mrs. Jenkins. "They play an important part in our lives. Who can tell me how we use numbers every day?"

"Numbers tell where we live," says Nora. "I live at 9 Grove Street."

"Numbers help people call us on the phone," says Timothy. "My phone number is 555-8416."

"Numbers say what time we have to do things," says Fritz. "I have to go to bed at eight o'clock."

"Very good," says Mrs. Jenkins.

Look at the pictures on the next page and say how we use these numbers.

The Next Step

What is the number of your house or apartment? What is your phone number? How old are you?

At snack time, Mrs. Jenkins brings out a big bowl of fruit. "We have two red apples and two green apples," she says to the class. "Can anyone tell me how many apples we have altogether?"

"I know!" says Nora. "We have four apples. But I'd like a plum, please."

"I'd like two plums, please," says Doris. "I'm hungry!"

"Okay," says Mrs. Jenkins. "If I give one plum to Nora and two plums to Doris, how many plums will they have altogether?"

"We'll have three," says Nora.

"You're right!" says Mrs. Jenkins. "There are three bananas in the bowl, and Fritz brought a banana from home. If he adds his banana to the bowl, how many bananas will we have?" Do you know?

Look at the pictures on the next page and try to answer the questions.

 The Next Step

Place five objects (pennies, jelly beans, crayons, or whatever you'd like) on the table in front of you. Now add two more objects. How many objects do you have? Add one more object. How many objects do you have now?

Yoko has three crayons.
Timothy has two crayons.
How many crayons do
they have altogether?

The Franks each have
one soccer ball. How many
soccer balls do they have
altogether?

Charles has four balloons.
Nora has one balloon.
How many balloons do they
have altogether?

9

 = 1¢  = 5¢  = 10¢  = 25¢

"Look what I brought in for show-and-tell!" says Fritz. "My piggy bank."

Fritz uncorks his piggy bank and spills all of his coins onto the table.

"You have saved a lot of money, Fritz," says Mrs. Jenkins. "Does anyone know what the different coins are called?"

"This is a penny," says Timothy. "It's worth one cent."

"And this is a nickel," says Claude. "It's worth five cents."

"This is a dime," says Yoko. "It's worth ten cents."

"And this is a quarter," says Charles. "It's worth twenty-five cents."

"Very good!" says Mrs. Jenkins. "Let's see if we can separate all of the coins into piles of pennies, nickels, dimes, and quarters."

Look at Fritz's coins. Point to all the pennies. Now point to all the nickels. Point to all the dimes. Now point to all the quarters. How many of each coin does Fritz have?

The Next Step

Borrow a pile of coins from an adult and try to separate them into piles of pennies, nickels, dimes, and quarters. Do you remember how much each kind of coin is worth? How many of each kind of coin do you have?

11

The students in Mrs. Jenkins's class are making crafts.

"I'm making a necklace for my mother," says Yoko.

"That's pretty," says Timothy. "I'm making a bookmark for my father. What are you making, Nora?"

"I'm making a crown with jewels on it," says Nora. "Look, I'm a princess!"

Look at the necklace Yoko is making. What color noodle should come next in the pattern?

Look at the bookmark Timothy is making. Which shape should come next in the pattern?

Look at the crown Nora is making. Which jewel should come next in the pattern?

The Next Step

You can make your own macaroni bead necklace. Ask an adult to get a box of noodles for you. (Make sure the noodles have holes so you can string your necklace.) Paint the uncooked noodles different colors and let them dry. Then string them onto a piece of yarn in a pattern. When you're done, tie the ends of the yarn together and wear your necklace.

During art time, Mrs. Jenkins brings out lots of sheets of different-colored paper.

"Blue is my favorite color," says Doris.

"Mine, too!" says Nora.

"Our favorite color is green," say the Franks.

"Mine is red," says Yoko.

"Here is what I want you to do," says Mrs. Jenkins. "Everyone take one sheet of paper of their favorite color. We'll take turns putting them on the board, arranging all the sheets of the same color in a line. When everyone is finished we'll have a graph that shows what the most and least popular colors are in our classroom."

Can you tell what the most popular color is in Mrs. Jenkins's class?

The Next Step

You can make your own favorite-color graph. Ask your friends and family members what their favorite colors are, then put pieces of colored paper on a board the way the students in Mrs. Jenkins's class did. Which color is the most popular?

Look at the color graph Mrs. Jenkins's class made. Which color do the most students like the best? Which color do the fewest students like the best? How many students like red the best?

1   2   3   4   5   6   7   8   9   10

Mrs. Jenkins's class is lining up in pairs to go out to recess.

"I'm going to give each of us a number," says Mrs. Jenkins.

Timothy is number 1 and Yoko is number 2. Fritz is number 3 and Doris is number 4. Nora is number 5 and Charles is number 6. The Franks are numbers 7 and 8. Claude is number 9 and Mrs. Jenkins is number 10.

"Now," says Mrs. Jenkins, "I want everyone on Yoko's side of the line to say their numbers in order."

"Two," says Yoko.

"Four," says Doris.

"Six," says Charles.

"Eight," says Frank.

"Ten," says Mrs. Jenkins. "Great job! We just counted to ten by twos, using every other number."

Can you count to ten by twos? Try it with the numbers written on the top of this page.

The Next Step

Can you count by twos all the way up to twenty?

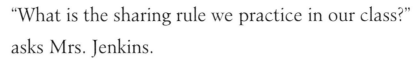

"What is the sharing rule we practice in our class?"
asks Mrs. Jenkins.

"Share and share alike," everyone says.

"That's right," says Mrs. Jenkins. "If two of
you were sharing the cookies on my plate
so you each get the same number of
cookies, how many would each of you get?"

"We'd each get two," says Claude.

"Right!" says Mrs. Jenkins. "And if two of you were
sharing so you each get the same number of these
graham crackers, how many would each of you get?"

"Three?" asks Timothy.

"Yes," says Mrs. Jenkins. "You're right."

Look at the pictures on the next page. Which show
objects divided in half? Which do not?

The Next Step

If you were going to share these apples with a friend, how many would each
of you get if you shared and shared alike?

During playtime, Fritz is playing with four toy trucks.
Doris wants to play with the trucks, too.

"Fritz, can I play with one of the trucks?" she asks.

"Yes," Fritz says. "You can have the red one."

"Thank you!" says Doris.

If Fritz has four trucks and he gives one truck to Doris, how many trucks will he have left?

The Next Step

Practice taking away. Get five objects and give two of them to someone else. How many do you have left? Now give one more to someone else. How many do you have left? Give one more to someone else. How many do you have left now?

Yoko is folding origami birds.
"Yoko, those are so beautiful!"
says Timothy. "Can I have one?"
"You can have two!" says Yoko.
If Yoko has four birds and she
gives two to Timothy, how many
birds will she have left?

Charles is looking at picture books.
"Charles, I want to look at books, too.
Can we share?" asks Nora.
"Okay," says Charles. "You can have
these two and I'll look at this one."
"Thank you!" says Nora.
If Charles has three books and he
gives two to Nora, how many books
does he have left?

1 2 3 4 5 6 7 8 9 10

The school day is nearly over.

"We almost forgot to feed the fish!" say the Franks. "It is our job today."

"There is still time," says Mrs. Jenkins.

"You may go feed the fish now."

"There are so many fish!" says Frank.

"I can count them all."

Can you? Look at the fish tank and the number line on the top of the page.

Point to the number that shows:

how many yellow fish are in the tank.

how many red fish are in the tank.

how many blue fish are in the tank.

how many big fish are in the tank.

how many little fish are in the tank.

 **The Next Step**

If Mrs. Jenkins adds one more red fish, how many red fish will be in the tank? If one big fish jumps out of the tank, how many big fish will be left?

22

Letter to Parents and Educators

The early years are a dynamic and exciting time in a child's life, a time in which children acquire language, explore their environment, and begin to make sense of the world around them. In the preschool and kindergarten years parents and teachers have the joy of nurturing and promoting this continued learning and development. The books in the *Get Set for Kindergarten!* series are designed to help in this wonderful adventure.

The activities in this book were created to be developmentally appropriate and geared toward the interests, needs, and abilities of pre-kindergarten and kindergarten children. After each activity, a suggestion is made for "The Next Step," an extension of the skill being practiced. Some children may be ready to take the next step; others may need more time.

Adding It Up is designed to extend and expand the young child's developing understanding of concepts and operations in mathematics. The activities in this book build upon knowledge of counting, shapes, patterns, and measuring so children can use what they already know to further develop their mathematical awareness and ability. Simple addition and subtraction activities are also included to guide children through the reasoning underlying each operation.

Throughout the early years, children need to be surrounded by language and learning and love. Those who nurture and educate young children give them a gift of immeasurable value that will sustain them throughout their lives.

John F. Savage, Ed.D.
Educational Consultant